SOLDIER'S PROMISE

A SWEET MILITARY ROMANCE

HONOR VALLEY ROMANCES
BOOK TWO

SHANAE JOHNSON

THOSE JOHNSON GIRLS

CHAPTER ONE

"Sarah needs to start thinking about settling down."

The words were spoken in a hushed tone. But it was the kind of hushed tone that could be heard over loudspeakers in a dance club on Saturday night. In other words, the words were hissed out at full volume and carried to the next room, where the aforementioned Sarah heard her mother's words loud and clear.

"Well, I don't know who's left for her to marry. She's dated every man in town."

Those words were from her sister Marjorie, who didn't even bother to affect a stage whisper. But that was Marjorie. She came out of the womb shouting and pointing a finger at her older sister, insisting it was Sarah's fault her labor had taken forty-eight hours.

"Whatever happened to that nice fellow she was seeing last Christmas?"

Leave it to her father to play the peacemaker in the family. Too bad the man he'd brought up had been more interested in sitting quietly in a boat all day with her dad fishing than in spending actual time with Sarah. Jerry was likely still sitting on the lake since he stood her up on their last date.

"Well, she can't show up to the family reunion alone," her mother stage-whispered as if there was anyone in the town that didn't know why Sarah was going to be made to feel uncomfortable at her own family's gathering.

"Yeah," snorted her sister. "That would just be pathetic."

"You know, my fishing buddy Marvin has been bringing his nephew around on the lake the past couple of weekends. I could see if he might be interested in our girl."

"Oh, but you know what, Lonnie Jensen is back in town. He just moved back into his mother's basement after his divorce."

Sarah had had enough. Unfortunately, she had to keep her cool for at least another thirty seconds as her family discussed, ad nauseam, her failures in her romantic life. Having Mrs. Garland, a known gossip in the small town of Honor Valley, hear every word her mom, dad, and sister said behind her back was just icing on the cake.

But even after Sarah wrapped up Mrs. Garland's weekly order of pink peonies and baby's breath, Mrs. Garland took longer than thirty seconds to make her way to the door. Finally, the doorbell over the top of Hayes Flower Shop jingled, and Sarah was able to march into the back room where her family held court over the problem of her love life.

Their voices filled the air, their words piercing her ears and stirring a mix of annoyance and frustration within her. It was a scene she had witnessed far too many times before, their well-intentioned but misguided attempts to find her the perfect match.

Her mother's concerned voice rose above the rest. "Sarah hasn't had the best track record in men. But at least Bernie could keep a steady job. I don't see how she let that one go."

"Maybe because he cheated on me with my cousin," Sarah said from the doorway.

Not one of her family members had the decency to jump or flinch at her sudden presence.

"Janet is going to be at the family reunion," said her sister. "And she's bringing Bernie."

As if Sarah didn't know that. She'd been thinking up ways of getting out of going to it. But she'd have an easier job hitching a ride on the next mission to Mars.

"It could be the perfect opportunity for them to get back together." Her mother clapped her hands together, her eyes going as big as flying saucers.

The possibility of Sarah getting back together with her ex-boyfriend was as likely as the chance of a Martian parking his flying spaceship on Main Street.

"I think she needs to move on," said her dad. "Come fishing with me next weekend, sweetheart. There's a young man I think you'd enjoy meeting."

"I don't want to date." Sarah finally spoke up, hoping to put an end to the conversation.

"You're going to wait for Janet to screw this up?" asked her sister. "We all know she can't hold on to a man."

"I have moved on."

Her mother's eyes lit up. Her father's mouth turned down in disappointment. Marjorie sniffed, looking doubtful. Then she looked down at her phone.

"I'm not dating," said Sarah. "I'm taking a break from relationships. And that includes being set up. So don't try it."

The silence from the three of them did not bode well. But Sarah was done arguing. She knew she was wasting her breath.

"It's a good thing you have moved on," Marjorie said, her gaze still on her phone. "Because it looks like I was wrong about Janet and Bernie."

Sarah's heart gave a kick. Not at the possibility of her getting back together with Bernie. That ship had sailed, sunk, been excavated and stripped for parts. She would just be glad she wouldn't have to miss her family reunion. She loved her crazy family and didn't want to miss out.

But when Marjorie held up her phone, Sarah took one and then another step back, trying to put distance between herself and her family. She kept walking until she was back in the flower shop. Then she was out the door. She didn't stop walking until she was down the street in her best friend's coffee shop with a warm mug of tea in her hands.

"Engaged?" asked Aria.

"But it's only been two months," protested Grace, her second-best friend.

Sarah buried her face in the warm brew and gulped it down. She couldn't feel the burn, but she felt the sting. She had moved on, but the sight of the ring on Janet's fat fingers on the social media post was a bruising punch to the gut.

She wanted to scream, to cry, to lash out at the unfairness of it all. But instead, she took a deep breath and tried to steady herself. "How could he do this to me?"

"Sarah, I'm so sorry."

Sarah shrugged, feeling numb. "It's fine. I've moved on," she said, even though she knew it wasn't entirely true.

"I never liked that Janet," said Grace.

The vehemence in her words was enough to crack the tiniest smile from Sarah. Grace loved everyone and never had a bad thing to say about anyone. That was as good as cursing Janet out for the town librarian.

Sarah didn't reply, lost in her own thoughts. The news of her ex's engagement had stirred up old wounds, reminding her of the pain and betrayal she had felt when she had caught him cheating.

"I just don't understand why people cheat," she said finally. "It's like they don't care about the other person's feelings at all."

"Some people are just selfish," said Aria. "But don't let this make you lose faith in love. There are still good guys out there."

Sarah smiled faintly, knowing that her friend meant well. Aria had just found the love of her life while cleaning up the local beach. She and Jace's relationship had started off rocky, with Aria still reeling from years of dealing with her ex-husband's PTSD symptoms. But she and her retired serviceman were seeking the help they needed separately as well as together, determined to make their relationship work.

A twinge of jealousy bit at the inside of Sarah's lip as she swallowed down the dregs in her teacup. She had once believed in love, in long-term relationships, in the idea of forever. But after what had happened with her ex, those beliefs had been shattered.

Sarah couldn't shake the feeling that she was destined to be alone. She didn't want to be hurt again, to risk her heart on someone who might betray her trust.

But as she looked out the window, watching

the world go by, a small part of her couldn't help wondering if maybe, just maybe, there was someone out there who would prove her wrong. Someone who would show her that love was still worth believing in.

CHAPTER TWO

*A*lex sat in the crowded briefing room. His broad shoulders spanned beyond the width of the conference room chair. Not that he rested his back against the cushioned office furniture. His military training wouldn't let him chill during an operation meeting. He remained on alert, listening to the chatter of his colleagues as they waited for their assignments for the upcoming event. Instead of the click and snapping of weapons being readied and assembled, the room was filled with the sounds of shuffling papers and the hum of whispered conversations.

He picked up on the conversations. Though he wished he could tune them out. Nothing anyone was saying had anything to do with the mission at hand. Not Tracy anticipating her first weekend away with her boyfriend. Not Maya learning that the bun in the oven she was carrying was a little girl. Not Ayman's decision over which grill to buy for his backyard barbecue on Saturday.

"So what are you doing this weekend, Alex?" asked one of his colleagues, a young woman with blonde hair and bright blue eyes. "Aside from the base cookout."

Right, the base cookout. It was something Alex was not planning on attending. But it looked like he wouldn't have a choice if he wanted to get ahead in his position.

"Got a hot date lined up?" the guy across from him—what was his name again?—was asking.

Alex shook his head, his expression neutral. "No, I'll be working on the Stringer project to try to get us ahead," he said, hoping to shut down any further questioning.

But his colleague persisted. "Come on, Alex, you've got to get out there and meet some new people. You can't stay a loner forever."

Alex bristled at the comment but tried to keep his cool. "I'm not a loner. I just have other priorities right now."

And dating wasn't one of them. There were too many variables in dating.

His colleagues had been teasing him about his single status, encouraging him to put himself out there and find someone special. They spoke of the joys of companionship and the excitement of romance. But for Alex, dating felt like a calculated risk—one he wasn't quite ready to take.

There was an unpredictable nature to relationships, emotional vulnerabilities, and the uncertainty that came with opening oneself up to another person. As a military intelligence officer, he had learned to analyze risks, assess probabilities, and make informed decisions. Yet when it came to matters of the heart, the variables seemed too numerous, the potential consequences too great.

He couldn't deny the allure of companionship and the warmth of a genuine connection, but he also knew the demanding nature of his work. His dedication to duty had often consumed his time and energy, leaving little room for personal pursuits. And with the lingering shadows of his past experiences, he felt a certain apprehension about diving into the world of dating.

As he glanced around the conference room, he

noted that every single person assembled was either married or in a committed relationship. They were all smiling and happily entwined with another person. Still, he didn't think he was missing out. His gaze shifted back to the intelligence reports, the redacted lines that symbolized hidden dangers and potential threats. It reminded him of the real risks he dealt with every day, the weight of the responsibility he carried.

Alex took a deep breath, his resolve firming. For now, he believed he needed to focus on his work, to ensure the safety and security of those under his watch. He was dedicated to his mission, committed to protecting others. The risks he'd faced in his military career were calculated, measured, and understood—a realm where he felt more in control. Now, as a civilian, those lessons carried over.

When his boss entered the room, Alex was the only one who sat up straight in his chair. Not that he'd been slouching as they waited for the commander to enter. He had to tell himself to stay in his seat and not rise, as it wasn't customary for civilian employees to salute.

Still, old habits died hard. Alex tilted his chin in an acknowledgement of respect to Commander

Mitchell. Not that the man noticed. He was busy greeting each person by name. Going so far as to ask after their health and their loved ones.

Alex held himself still. He willed his foot not to tap on the floor, but his impatience was growing—well, impatient. He was preoccupied with his desire to advance in his job. He had been with the military for years, but after an injury in combat left him medically discharged, he was struggling to find his place in civilian life.

Commander Mitchell took his seat in the middle of the conference table. Something that irked Alex. The man should be sitting at the head, but he had a Knights of the Roundtable way of leading that left Alex twitchy. Alex also noted that his boss had skipped over making any niceties with him.

As the commander started handing out assignments, Alex rested his hands on his knees to aid in keeping them still. He'd been assigned basic analysis tasks so far. What he wanted was to be a part of the decision-making process based on the data he analyzed.

"Tracy, you've been doing an excellent job with your analysis reports. I think it's time you take on more decision-making roles here."

Tracy grinned her delight at the announcement.

"I know you're headed out of town this week-end," the commander continued. "Give your reports to Alex to manage while you're away."

And with that, the commander closed the meeting.

Alex sat in his chair long after the room cleared. He was so stunned that when he finally roused, he found that his shoulders were touching the wings of the office chair's back. Slowly, he rose. He put one foot in front of the other until he was outside the commander's door.

Alex cleared his throat, feeling his nerves start to fray. "Commander Mitchell, I was hoping we could talk about my career goals," he said, trying to keep his voice steady. "It is clear that I've been passed over for some of the bigger assignments lately, and I would like to understand what I'm doing wrong in my current position to warrant this."

Commander Mitchell frowned slightly, looking thoughtful. "Well, Alex, it's not that I don't think you're capable," he said slowly. "It's just that some of the other employees have a bit more...stability, let's say. They're in committed relationships, and I know that they're less likely to jump ship if a better opportunity comes along."

Alex had to run the man's words through his brain a few times. For such an analytical person, it was hard to get the meanings to compute.

"Respectfully, sir, I don't see what my relationship status has to do with my performance," he said, his voice firm. "I'm just as dedicated to this job as anyone else, and I don't think my personal life should be a factor in determining my career prospects."

His boss raised an eyebrow, looking slightly surprised. "Could you see yourself staying in Honor Valley for the long-term?"

"I can see myself staying with this base if there is room for advancement."

Commander Mitchell leaned forward, his voice carrying a tinge of concern. "Alex, you've been a valuable asset to this base, and your performance has been exceptional. But I can't ignore the fact that you haven't fully integrated into the community. It's important for us to have employees who understand the town, who can build relationships with the locals."

"I've been focused on my duties and the demands of my position. I haven't made the effort to connect beyond the base." Alex's jaw tensed as he struggled to find the right words. "Commander, with all due respect, I joined the military to serve my country and protect its interests. While I understand the importance of community engagement, I believe my dedication to my duties on the base should be the primary factor in evaluating my readiness for advancement."

Commander Mitchell sighed, his expression a mix of understanding and frustration. "Alex, I'm not asking you to put community engagement above your duties. I'm simply saying that a well-rounded officer understands the dynamics of the environment they operate in. Being connected to the community can enhance your effectiveness as a leader."

Alex's brow furrowed as he pondered the commander's words. The idea of dedicating time to community events and local initiatives seemed daunting, as if it would divert his focus from his primary responsibilities.

"How about this?" said the commander. "I'll put you in charge of decor for the base picnic this weekend."

"Decor?"

"Streamers. Balloons. Flowers. Think festive. Think you can handle that mission?"

Alex had been a top tier officer in the military for years. He'd put together and pulled apart tactical missions. And now he was being put on the decorating party. Maybe it was time to look at another job after all.

CHAPTER THREE

Sarah stepped into her family's flower shop, glad to be surrounded by the sweet scent of blossoms and greenery. She was also glad to be alone. Her parents were at the rec center this morning for a cutthroat game of pickleball with some of their best friends from childhood. Sarah made sure to stay far away from that, as there could very likely be blood on the floor after the friendly match.

Her sister was still asleep. With it being the summer, Marjorie was on college break. Though she made it a point not to attend any classes before noon.

The doorbell dinged. Sarah looked up to see

Grace. Grace's eyes held a mix of sympathy and determination, her steps purposeful as she made her way toward Sarah. Her friend tugged at the cardigan around her shoulders with one hand. In the other hand, she held a small package.

Grace held the book up high as though it were a winning lottery ticket. "I've got just the thing for your dilemma."

Curiosity mingled with weariness in Sarah's expression as she accepted the small, wrapped package from Grace. It wasn't cold enough to be a tub of ice cream, the normal cure for a bad breakup.

"What's this?"

Grace's smile widened as she gestured to the package. "Open it. I thought you could use a little distraction from all the chaos with your ex."

Sarah carefully unwrapped the package, revealing a paperback book adorned with a colorful cover depicting a couple lost in an embrace. The title read *Faking Love*. Sarah's eyebrows knitted together as she read it aloud.

Grace's eyes sparkled with anticipation. "It's a romance novel, Sarah. The perfect escape from reality, at least for a little while. It's about a woman who hires a fake boyfriend to save face after her ex moves on. I thought it might help take your mind off things."

Sarah let out a soft sigh, her gaze lingering on the book's cover. She appreciated Grace's thoughtful gesture, but deep down, she knew that escaping into a fictional world of fake relationships wouldn't solve her problems.

"I know you mean well, but I don't think a romance novel can fix what's happened. It's not as simple as hiring a fake boyfriend to save face."

Sarah headed to the flowers lined up on the wall near the door, leaving the book on the glass surface.

"Sometimes, losing yourself in a story can provide a temporary respite from reality," said Grace. "It's not about finding a solution but about finding solace."

Sarah's shoulders slumped, a mix of sadness and frustration settling in her chest. She appreciated Grace's attempt to lift her spirits, but the truth was, no amount of fictional tales could erase the hurt and betrayal she had experienced.

"Right now, I think I just need some time to process everything. Maybe a tub of ice cream and a good cry."

"You still have feelings for Bernie?"

Sarah wrinkled her nose. "Not at all. I'm mourning my Aunt Cathy's potato salad. I'm going to miss out at the reunion."

"Maybe invite one of your male friends to be your companion, not necessarily your date."

"My family will pounce and start making wedding announcements for anyone I bring. Besides, my family knows everyone in this town."

When she turned, she collided with someone, and a bouquet of flowers went flying.

"I'm so sorry," a deep voice said.

Sarah looked up to see a tall, muscular man with short-cropped dark hair and piercing blue eyes. He wore casual clothing but looked handsome and put-together.

Their eyes met, and Sarah felt a jolt of electricity shoot through her. She didn't know who this man was, but she couldn't deny the sudden rush of attraction she felt.

"It's okay," she said, blushing. "I wasn't looking where I was going."

"Neither was I, apparently. Let me help you with that."

Together, they gathered the scattered flowers and rearranged them into a new bouquet. As he handed it to her, their hands brushed, and Sarah felt her heart skip a beat.

"Thanks," she said, her voice barely above a whisper.

She stole a quick glance at the man beside her, her eyes widening in surprise. He had a commanding presence, his muscular frame emanating strength and resilience. His short-cropped dark hair accentuated his chiseled features, and his piercing blue eyes held a hint of intensity. There was a scar above his left eyebrow. Maybe it was a mark of battles fought. He had the stern face of a warrior. Sarah couldn't help but be drawn to the ruggedness it represented.

She noticed the strong, confident aura that surrounded him, like someone who had faced challenges head-on and emerged stronger. In that moment, she couldn't deny the allure he possessed.

"No harm done. Accidents happen, especially when there are flowers involved."

"I apologize once again for the collision. I hope the flowers still bring joy to someone's day."

"Are you looking to bring someone joy today? Is that why you stopped into the flower shop?"

"We're having a picnic at my job. On the base. I've been put in charge of decorations."

"I'm surprised your girlfriend isn't in here to help you."

Sarah gave the man her back and looked to see where her mother had materialized from. But only Grace stood in the room, her lips stretched in a smirk. Sarah's mother was nowhere to be found. Those prying words had come directly from Sarah's own mouth.

"I don't have a girlfriend," he admitted. "Seems like everyone at my work is in a relationship except for me."

Grace spoke up, a hint of mischief in her eyes. "Do you want a girlfriend?"

The man who had to be a soldier looked over at her, startled. "What? No, I didn't say that. I'm too focused on work right now."

His gaze landed on the romance book on the counter.

"But it might be the thing to get people off my back and get the promotion I want." He smiled wryly as he fingered the cover of the embracing couple. Then he gave himself a shake.

"I think the two of you could help each other out," said Grace.

"Grace," Sarah admonished.

But Grace ignored her friend. "Sarah needs a date to her family reunion this weekend. You think a relationship might get you the career advancement you want. Sounds like the perfect foundation for a fake dating agreement."

CHAPTER FOUR

When Alex strode into the flower shop, his shoulders had been squared and his posture erect, ready to tackle the tasks of the day. He wasn't ready for a relationship to prove to his boss that he was integrating into the community, but he figured he could purchase a few balloons and bouquets for the picnic. But as he made his way through the delicate blooms, his gaze fixed ahead, his entire stance faltered when his shoulder collided with an unexpected force.

Stumbling slightly, Alex's confident stride came to a momentary halt as he turned to face the person he had bumped into. His eyes widened as they met the captivating gaze of the woman he had inadvertently collided with. Her beauty was a sight to behold, a mesmerizing combination of grace and warmth that caught him off guard.

In that moment, Alex felt a shift in his usually unwavering resolve. Her sparkling eyes and that hint of a blush on her cheeks caused his heart to skip a beat. Her presence disrupted his forward march, making him question the path he had been so determined to follow.

What was he doing here? In a flower shop?

"I think the two of you could help each other out," said another woman standing at the counter.

Alex glanced at this other woman. His heart beat steadily in his chest. He didn't have the same reaction to her as he did to the woman standing just beyond his reach.

"Sarah needs a date to her family reunion this weekend. You think a relationship might get you the career advancement you want. Sounds like the perfect foundation for a fake dating agreement."

"Please ignore my friend," said Sarah. "I think the dust from the library has finally gone to her head."

"It's the perfect solution," said the friend. "You get your family off your back, and he gets his boss and coworkers off his back."

Had Alex mentioned his boss and coworkers? His job? The promotion he wanted?

Oh yes, he had. He'd never spoken so openly about his issues at work. Except with his buddies, Jace and Mason. And those talks were only a few unintelligible grunts over beers on the beach.

"It's a foolproof plan," said the friend.

There was no such thing as a foolproof plan. As a military intelligence officer, Alex approached the notion of fake dating Sarah with a calculated and analytical mindset. He acknowledged the ploy was a pragmatic approach to navigate the complexities of personal and professional dynamics. It offered a mutually beneficial arrangement that could alleviate the pressures faced by both him and Sarah while concurrently furthering their individual goals. But the plan carried some inherent risks, such as the potential for emotional entanglements and complications.

"Grace, stop. You're making him uncomfortable."

But that was just it. For all the calculations he did in his mind, including the inherent risks, Alex wasn't uncomfortable at the idea of spending time with Sarah.

"You work at the base, right?" asked Grace.

When Alex nodded, she continued. "There's a picnic going on this weekend, right? I know because the commander's wife is a member of Friends of the Library. If you take Sarah to the picnic on Sunday, and she takes you to her family reunion on Saturday, it'll solve both your problems."

Alex ran his fingers through his short-cropped hair, contemplating the proposal that could help him secure his desired promotion. His eyes flickered toward Sarah, who was engrossed in arranging a bouquet nearby. The way she effortlessly handled the delicate blooms, her fingers dancing across the petals.

"And there's the added benefit of Aunt Cathy's potato salad," said Grace.

"Aunt Cathy does make the best potato salad," said Sarah, her voice gone dreamy.

"Although potato salad sounds really good, I don't know if it's a good idea," Alex said. "I don't think I'm boyfriend material."

"Then you're exactly my type." Sarah laughed.

It was a self-deprecating sound. Alex couldn't understand why she would belittle herself. From what he could see, the woman was perfection.

"Her last boyfriend cheated on her," said Grace. "Now he's engaged to her cousin."

"Sounds like a boy, not a man. And an idiot at that."

Sarah gasped as her gaze lifted to his.

"Sorry." Alex lowered his gaze as well as his tone. He didn't know where that vehemence had come from. "I didn't mean to offend you."

"I'm not offended at all." Sarah paused, studying him for a moment. "I changed my mind. I think we should do this. I think a fake boyfriend is the best way to get my parents off my back."

"And have potato salad," said Alex.

"Definitely. I want the potato salad. You'll get some too, and you'll love it."

The next day, Alex entered the base in a daze. He couldn't believe what had happened at the flower shop. He had agreed to a fake relationship with Sarah, a woman he barely knew. What was he thinking?

He had been so caught up in his own professional issues that he didn't even consider the consequences of his actions on his personal issues. He knew he had been struggling with anxiety and PTSD since returning from his last mission, but he'd never expected it to affect his personal life this much.

The support group on base that met to discuss issues such as PTSD wouldn't be meeting until next weekend. So he wouldn't be able to explore his actions until then. Though he wasn't sure he wanted to. They would likely try and talk him out of this. Alex wasn't so sure he wanted to be talked out of spending time with Sarah.

As he sat at his desk, memories flooded back to him of the mission that went wrong. The screams of his fellow soldiers echoed in his ears as he watched them fall one by one. He could still feel the heat of the explosions and the taste of blood in his mouth.

It was no wonder he was having trouble with relationships. He couldn't even take care of himself, let alone someone else. How could he be what Sarah needed? Even just for a weekend?

As much as he didn't want to admit it, he was having doubts about this fake relationship. He didn't want to lead her on or hurt her in any way. But at the same time, he couldn't deny the attraction he felt toward her.

"Morning, Alex. Heard you met someone at the flower shop yesterday."

Alex looked up to find Commander Mitchell leaning over the partition to his desk.

"How did you-"

"Small town," said the commander. "I've got a project I need someone to lead, and I was thinking you'd be perfect for the job," his boss said, handing him a folder.

Alex was surprised. He'd been hoping for a chance to prove himself, but he hadn't expected it to happen so soon. But then he realized his boss was assuming that he and Sarah were dating.

"Thanks, sir. I'll take a look."

As his boss walked away, Alex opened the folder and scanned the contents. It wasn't a huge project, but it was one that would require him to work closely with others and make important decisions. He knew he was up for the challenge, but he also knew this folder had only landed in his lap because of Sarah. Or at least what his boss assumed was going on between him and Sarah.

He sighed and leaned back in his chair, running a hand through his short hair. He couldn't believe he was going through with this. But he also couldn't deny that he wanted that promotion. Maybe this was his chance to prove himself, to show that he was more than just a soldier struggling to adapt to civilian life.

He took a deep breath and resolved to do his best, even if it meant pretending to be someone he wasn't. He just hoped Sarah was up for the challenge, too.

CHAPTER FIVE

*S*arah could feel her nerves building up as they approached the large, white tent that had been set up in her grandparents' back-yard. Her family reunion was in full swing, and she wasn't sure if she was ready for it. She couldn't shake the feeling that their carefully constructed cover would crumble under the scrutiny of her relatives. She glanced over at Alex, who seemed surprisingly composed, and wondered how he managed to maintain such calm amidst the chaos.

Alex, standing tall and exuding confidence, took a deep breath before addressing Sarah, his voice steady and reassuring. "We stick to our story and say as little as possible. I'll take the lead and deflect any unwanted attention. Just follow me and remember the key details we've discussed."

Sarah nodded, her mind filled with doubts and worries. She had always felt like the black sheep of her family, the one who didn't quite fit into their traditional values and expectations. The pressure of maintaining the charade was overwhelming, and she feared that her nerves would betray them.

"You look really pretty, by the way."

Sarah's cheeks turned pink as she looked up at him. "Thank you," she said softly. "And you look very handsome."

Handsomer than any of her ex-boyfriends. More put together as well. No one was going to believe this man was interested in her. They'd see right through the façade. But even worse, Bernie and Janet would be witnesses to her humiliation.

"Ready?" Alex asked.

"Yeah." If she was gonna go out, she was going to do it in a blaze of glory.

As they made their way closer to the tent, Sarah could hear the sound of laughter and chatter growing louder. The smell of barbecue and fresh cut grass filled the air, and Sarah could feel her stomach churn with nerves.

"Are you okay?" Alex asked, squeezing her hand gently.

"I'm just nervous," Sarah admitted. "My family can be a lot to handle."

Just as they reached the entrance of the tent, a woman with curly red hair approached them with a big smile. "Sarah! It's so good to see you!" she said, pulling Sarah into a tight hug.

Sarah hugged her back, feeling a sense of relief wash over her. "It's good to see you too, Aunt Mary," she said with a smile.

"And who's this?" Aunt Mary asked, looking at Alex curiously.

"This is Alex," Sarah said, introducing him. "He's my boyfriend."

"Boyfriend? Really?"

Sarah didn't like her aunt's tone. The woman had been through three husbands in her lifetime. She'd outlived them all and was actively looking for number four. Sarah couldn't determine if Aunt Mary's pitch was incredulous that Sarah could snag a man like Alex, or if she was assessing how she could snare him for herself.

Alex rested his palm on Sarah's low back. She might have imagined it, but she would've sworn she felt a slight tremor in his fingertips as they landed on her person.

"So, Alex," Aunt Mary began, a twinkle in her eye, "how long have you and Sarah been dating?"

"It's a recent development," Alex replied smoothly.

"I had no idea. But I'm glad our girl bounced back after that nastiness with-"

"Mom. Dad. Hi," Sarah called over her aunt's head.

"Sarah, you're late," her mom nagged. "Who's this?"

"You don't know Sarah's new boyfriend?" asked Aunt Mary.

"New...what?"

Already the plan was hitting a snag. They should've introduced Alex to her parents first. But there just hadn't been time for it.

"It's nice to finally meet you, Mrs. Hayes." Alex reached out a hand to her mother. When she gave it to him, he flipped her wrist and pressed a kiss to her knuckles.

"Oh." Her mother blushed.

"I didn't realize Sarah was dating," said Marjorie, her brows raised.

"That's because we wanted to keep it private for a while," said Sarah.

"Well, I'm just glad you found someone," said Aunt Mary. "You've been single for far too long."

It had only been a couple of months. But to her family, it was a lifetime.

"Come on, Alex. Let's go and find a table so we can get you something to eat."

"You did promise me potato salad."

"Aunt Cathy makes the world's best potato salad."

"He should also try my tuna casserole," said Aunt Mary.

Sarah would be deterring Alex from the toxic dish that everyone in her family knew to stay away from.

As they walked away, Aunt Mary followed in their wake, continuing to pepper them with questions. Others gathered around as she asked about their future plans and whether they had talked about marriage.

Alex kept a smile on his face. He answered each of her questions without actually answering them. His responses were vague with few details. But each seemed to satisfy her family. Sarah had a mind to start taking notes on these tactics.

"We're just taking it one day at a time, Aunt Mary. Maybe after a year or two, we'll talk about getting a dog."

Sarah giggled at Alex's response, feeling grateful for his quick wit.

Aunt Mary laughed too, charmed by Alex's easygoing personality. "Oh, I like this one, Sarah. He's a keeper," she said, patting Alex on the arm.

Alex smiled at her. "Thanks, Aunt Mary. I think Sarah's a keeper too," he said, looking over at Sarah and squeezing her hand.

Sarah's heart fluttered at Alex's words, feeling a warmth spread through her chest. She knew it was all fake, but in that moment, it felt real. She found herself looking forward to the rest of the day with Alex by her side.

Sarah took a deep breath as she led Alex into the crowded backyard of her family's reunion. She had always felt like the black sheep of the family, with her more modern values and independent nature. But with Alex by her side, she felt a little more secure.

She barely noticed that her ex was a no-show.

CHAPTER SIX

As Alex made his way through the lively outdoor party, his senses were heightened and his awareness on high alert. The sights, sounds, and smells of the event surrounded him, but his mind instinctively analyzed the situation, scanning for any potential risks or threats.

The boisterous laughter and animated conversations seemed to echo in his ears, a constant reminder of the unpredictable nature of large gatherings. He felt a sense of unease as his PTSD kept him on guard, always ready to assess any potential dangers lurking in his surroundings.

The array of unfamiliar faces, the mingling of voices, and the sheer magnitude of the crowd tested his ability to remain composed. The weight of their presence pressing upon him triggered a subtle anxiety deep within. Every interaction, every gesture, carried with it a level of uncertainty, a reminder that he was stepping into unfamiliar territory.

As Alex navigated the bustling party, his hand rested gently on the small of Sarah's back, a subtle touch that provided a steady reassurance amidst the whirlwind of emotions and stimuli. He felt a sense of grounding in her presence, her warmth seeping into his being like a protective shield against the chaos around them.

Sarah, with her vibrant energy and contagious smiles, had a way of electrifying his senses. Her mere presence made his heart race, filling him with a mixture of excitement and anticipation. But intertwined with that exhilaration was a profound sense of calm, a deep-seated peace that settled over his shoulders like a comforting embrace.

"I think it's working," she said. But when she said it, she leaned into him. Her bottom lip brushed the cone of his ear.

Alex's fingers, which had never left the small of her back, even while they were eating what turned out to be the most amazing potato salad he'd ever tasted, clenched. His thumb curled at the spot just above her sacrum. He'd heard of that space referred to as the seat of passion. With his fingers on it, he felt heat bloom between them.

"Yes," he breathed, his chin brushing against her cheek. "I think it's working, too."

Their eyes locked. Neither moved. He knew he didn't breathe. He didn't think she did either. He would've gulped down any exhale, given her his own if she needed to inhale.

Danger bells were ringing in his head. Normally, he would heed them. But honestly, those bells were ringing all the time these days. This was one situation Alex wasn't in a hurry to leave.

"Sarah, I need you."

Sarah was yanked away from him by her sister. Alex reached for her, but not quickly enough. She slipped through his fingers as she went to talk to her sister. But her gaze remained locked on him.

Alex forced himself to look away, yet he couldn't help but chastise himself for the wave of longing that washed over him. Amidst the cacophony of the gathering, his mind wrestled with conflicting thoughts. The agreement they had made, the notion that their relationship was merely a charade, loomed over him like a heavy shadow.

The magnetic pull between them intensified with each passing moment, drawing him closer into her orbit. His heart swelled with emotions he had long kept locked away, emotions that had been guarded by the fortress of his anxieties.

The desire to lean in, to capture her lips in a tender embrace, lingered at the edge of his thoughts. He restrained the urge, reminding himself of the boundaries they had set. He didn't want to risk jeopardizing the fragile equilibrium they had found, nor did he want to burden her with the weight of his insecurities.

So with a mix of longing and restraint, he vowed to protect her, even from him. He would only need to see her one more time to seal this deal. As the night wore on, he remained steadfast in his commitment to tread carefully, to shield her from the storm brewing within him.

As he observed her moving through the crowd, effortlessly engaging with her relatives and radiating a natural charm, he marveled at the contrast she brought to his world. Her vivacity and zest for life acted as a soothing balm to his weary soul, tempering the restlessness that often plagued him.

Just one more day with her. Just a few more hours in her presence. Then this would be all over. That was the deal.

As Alex contemplated the approaching end of their faux relationship, a bittersweetness settled within his heart. He had accomplished what they had set out to do—Sarah's family had eased off their matchmaking efforts, and tomorrow he would show a semblance of stability to further his career prospects.

It should have been a moment of triumph, a sense of relief washing over him. Yet his military-trained mind refused to let go of the incomplete mission. He couldn't shake the feeling that there was still more to be done, that he had only scratched the surface of what could be between him and Sarah. The notion of their upcoming final date loomed over him like an impending deadline, an expiration date on the connection they had formed.

It was a peculiar sensation, one he struggled to understand. He had always prided himself on his ability to compartmentalize, to view relationships as mere transactions, devoid of emotional entanglements. But Sarah had managed to disrupt that carefully constructed mindset, stirring emotions he had long suppressed in just a few hours.

The idea of parting ways, of severing the fragile bond they had nurtured didn't sit right with him. It seemed counterintuitive to cast aside something that brought him solace and stability. The prospect of returning to the solitary existence he had grown accustomed to left an ache in his chest.

But he reminded himself of the practicality of their arrangement. The mission was nearing its end, and he couldn't allow sentimentality to cloud his judgment. He had responsibilities, goals he needed to pursue, and he couldn't afford to lose focus.

CHAPTER SEVEN

"Kellie heard from Danielle who heard from cousin Trish that Bernie and Janet had a fight, and that's why they're not here at the reunion."

It took a moment for Sarah to track her sister's words. Mainly because she was too busy tracking Alex's movements. Had they just almost kissed a moment ago?

"Sarah? Did you hear me?"

"What? Yes, Bernie and Janet. Sure."

"You know what this means, right?"

Sarah looked at her sister dumbly.

"You could win him back."

"Why would I want to do that?"

"What? You're going to stay with the soldier?

The two of you are clearly pretending. I get why you're doing it, but I don't see his angle."

"You don't think a handsome guy like that who has his life together would go for someone like me?"

"No. That's not what I'm saying at all. He doesn't seem like the kind of guy who would stick around in Honor Valley, and you'd never leave home."

As Marjorie's words washed over Sarah, she felt a surge of frustration. The mention of her ex-boyfriend, Bernie, and the suggestion that she could rekindle a failed relationship left a bitter taste in her mouth. She had moved on from that chapter of her life, and the wounds of his betrayal were still too fresh.

Marjorie's comment also planted a seed of doubt in Sarah's mind. Could she truly forge something new with Alex, the man she was entangled with in this intricate web of lies? Was there a possibility for a genuine connection to grow from the foundation they had constructed? What if he didn't get the promotion? Would he leave?

Sarah glanced in Alex's direction, watching as he interacted with her family. He looked uncomfortable now that she was away from him. He was even a bit standoffish. He'd moved to a corner of the room, his body language clearly reading loner. But that wasn't how he'd been when he was with her.

Despite their arrangement being based on a fabrication, she couldn't deny the glimpses of authenticity she had witnessed in their time together. The way he made her feel seen, understood, and protected spoke volumes about the potential they held.

Maybe he was just a really good actor. That was probably it. And then there was what Marjorie predicted.

Would Alex stick around in town? Most former military who worked at the base didn't put down roots. The fear of being vulnerable, of opening herself up to the possibility of heartbreak once again, gnawed at her. The scars left by Bernie's betrayal were still healing, and she wasn't sure if she was ready to take that leap of faith.

Sarah knew the dynamics of her current situation were complicated. Her and Alex's connection had been built on the premise of a ruse, a charade meant to deceive those around them. How could something real and lasting emerge from such a foundation? Sarah wrestled with her conflicting emotions, torn between the safety of her walls and the longing for something genuine.

As Sarah's father approached, a warm smile played on his lips, and his eyes held a glimmer of approval. He extended a gentle hand, placing it on Sarah's shoulder, the warmth of his touch seeping into her being.

"I really like this Alex fellow," he said. "There's something about him, the way he carries himself, the way he looks at you. I can see that he cares deeply for you."

Sarah's heart swelled with a mix of emotions—gratitude for her father's support and under-standing but also a twinge of apprehension. She cast a glance at her mother, whose eyes also shim-mered with hope. Sarah knew that look, and she knew what was coming next.

"You and Alex make such a lovely couple. The grandbabies are going to be beautiful."

And here it was. Did it matter that they'd just met the guy? No, they just wanted a ring on their daughter's finger. It didn't matter who put it there.

"It's time to think about taking things to the next level," her mother was saying. "We should start planning a wedding, don't you think?"

Sarah's breath caught in her throat, the pressure from her mother's words nearly suffocating her. She wanted her family's happiness, but the idea of rushing into a commitment solely to meet their expectations felt overwhelming. She searched for the right words to express her own desires.

"Mom, I appreciate your enthusiasm, but we need to take things one step at a time," Sarah replied, her voice tinged with a hint of impatience. "What Alex and I have is still evolving, and rushing into something may not be the right course of action. Let's give it some time. Let it grow naturally."

Her mother's expression shifted from excitement to a mix of disappointment and nagging persistence. "But darling, you've been with him for a while now."

"It hasn't even been a week."

"You're not getting any younger, you know."

"Why aren't you having this conversation with Marjorie?"

"Marjorie's still in school. I'm hoping she'll snag a doctor on that campus. We need one in the family."

Sarah let out a groan and turned on her heel. But she didn't head in Alex's direction. She needed a moment to herself. One without family, or ex cheaters, or fake boyfriends.

When she felt someone at her back, she knew it was Alex. No one in her family would approach her that quietly, or without asking if she had an engagement ring yet. Sarah turned to look at him.

His normally composed demeanor seemed disrupted, his posture rigid and tense. His gaze met hers, a mixture of emotions flickering in his eyes. There was a vulnerability that Sarah hadn't seen before, a guardedness that made her heart ache. She could sense that he was holding something back, concealing the truth from her. The realization hit her like a wave, and a pang of doubt gnawed at her.

"Are you ready to run yet?" she asked, infusing humor into her voice.

He hesitated, his eyes darting away momentarily before settling back on her face. A conflicted expression played across his features, and Sarah's heart clenched in response.

How well did she really know him? Had their arrangement clouded her judgment, preventing her from truly understanding the depths of his heart?

"What's wrong?" she asked.

"I... Sarah, it's complicated," he began, his voice laced with a tinge of unease. He stepped closer to her, resting a hand on her shoulder.

She felt the shift in him before she saw it. Everything about him relaxed. The cool, confident man she'd arrived with was back.

"I just haven't been around this much family in a long time," he said. "It's a bit overwhelming."

"Things are winding down. We can start to say our goodbyes."

"Are you sure? I could just go. I don't want to keep you from your family."

"I got what I wanted—the potato salad."

"It was really good potato salad. I'm afraid you'll be disappointed tomorrow at the base picnic."

Sarah wasn't so sure. If she would get to stand this close to this man and feel the weight of his fingers pressing into her hip, she would risk the food poisoning from her Aunt Mary's casserole.

CHAPTER EIGHT

lex's car came to a stop in front of Sarah's house the next morning. He'd slept well, having gone to bed with a full belly, a lightness in his chest, and a tingle in his fingers from resting his hand on Sarah's hip and low back, brushing his fingers with her hand. His fingers clenched and unclenched as he surveyed her neighborhood.

Honor Valley might be a small town, but there was the potential for a threat anywhere. Alex couldn't suppress the instinctive habit ingrained within him. His eyes scanned the surroundings, assessing the neighborhood for potential blind areas.

As Alex's trained eyes scanned the neighborhood, he took note of the quaint houses lining the street. The houses exuded an air of familiarity and comfort, each with their neatly manicured lawns and welcoming front porches. Children played on the sidewalks, their laughter carrying through the air, painting the scene with an atmosphere of community.

He observed the neighbors going about their daily routines, their interactions suggesting a close-knit community. People exchanged friendly waves and conversations, their smiles genuine and warm. The sight of families walking their dogs and elderly couples strolling hand in hand added to the sense of peace and harmony.

His gaze shifted to the surrounding environment, taking in the nearby shops and establishments. A local coffee shop emanated the inviting aroma of freshly brewed coffee. The smells of home-cooked meals wafted from a small diner on the corner. The small library on the opposite corner displayed its colorful array of books, a testament to the town's appreciation for knowledge and culture.

The subtle sounds of nature Intertwined with the scene. Birds chirped in the trees, their melodies harmonizing with the rustle of leaves in the gentle breeze. The distant sound of a lawnmower, the occasional passing car, and the laughter of children playing at a nearby park completed the symphony of daily life in the neighborhood.

As Alex continued his assessment, he noticed the absence of any suspicious activities or signs of unrest. The atmosphere was tranquil, free from the shadows and threats that he had become accustomed to during his military service. It was a stark contrast to the battlefield, a reminder of the peaceful haven that small-town life could offer.

The sight before him spoke of safety, trust, and the potential for a different kind of existence. It presented an opportunity for him to let go of the constant vigilance and embrace a more peaceful way of life.

A sense of calm settled over Alex. The threat assessment he had performed was more of a habitual reflex than a genuine concern. He realized that Sarah's small town with its tight-knit community and serene ambiance provided a refuge from the chaos of the world.

As his gaze shifted back to Sarah's house, a realization washed over him—he had done it out of a growing concern for her safety. The weight of the revelation settled upon him, stirring a mix of emotions within his chest. The cold, calculated soldier he had once been was gradually making way for the man who cared for Sarah.

Just her safety, of course.

She was the key to getting what he wanted at work. His tingling fingers clenched and unclenched as he lifted his hand to knock on the door. His heart beat a little faster, a mix of anticipation and nervousness coursing through his veins. He was about to see Sarah again, to be in her presence, and the thought filled him with both excitement and trepidation.

Just as he was about to knock, the door swung open, revealing Sarah standing before him. Her eyes widened in surprise, and a smile tugged at the corners of her lips.

"Alex," she greeted him warmly, her voice filled with genuine happiness. "I didn't expect to see you so soon."

"I'm always early." He didn't say why he was always early.

As they stood there, their gazes locked, and the threat assessment he had conducted on his drive through her neighborhood seemed distant and trivial. The real risk, the vulnerability of allowing someone into his heart when his head was still messed up, became apparent.

Better to be done with this arrangement and then leave Sarah to find a man who thought about giving her flowers instead of a risk report. Although Alex wondered at the creativity of a man who would buy flowers for a woman whose family owned a flower shop. A guy like that couldn't possibly come with much tactical thinking. So he wouldn't be right for Sarah.

"Alex?"

"Yes?"

"Are you ready to go?"

He held out his arm to her. The moment her fingers touched his forearm, the wires got crossed in Alex's mind. He heard alarm bells in his head. But they weren't the kind that blared a tone of danger. They sounded more like wind chimes.

His head brushed a set of wind chimes hanging from the overhang on her porch. How had he missed that detail?

"You look beautiful."

Sarah blushed and smiled back, making Alex's heart skip a beat. He couldn't help but feel drawn to her, despite his anxieties about the day ahead.

"My coworkers can be a bit rowdy," he said as they drove to the base."But I think you'll like them."

"I'm sure I will. And don't worry; I can handle rowdy. You met my family last night."

He had, and after a time he'd retreated when she wasn't by his side. As soon as she had returned, so had his calm. His nerves had been on edge on the drive over, but the drive to the base, with Sarah by his side, was peaceful. Enjoyable even.

They rode mostly in silence. He supposed he should fill the void, but he didn't know what to talk about. His only topic of conversation for the last decade had been over mission reports and intel. What did one talk about on a fake date with their fake girlfriend?

By the time they arrived at the company picnic on the military base, Alex's mind was filled with self-doubt and insecurity. He observed his colleagues, each one seemingly confident and at ease in their own skin. They interacted effortlessly with their partners, displaying a level of charm and charisma that made Alex feel inadequate.

He watched as one of his coworkers, Mark, shared a lighthearted joke with his girlfriend, their laughter echoing across the picnic area. They seemed so carefree, so perfectly matched. Another colleague, Chris, held his wife's hand as they walked, their affectionate gestures capturing the attention of those around them. It was as if they were all living in a different world, where relationships bloomed effortlessly.

And Sarah was fitting right in with them. She picked up small talk easily. She moved from person to person, couple to couple, with ease. Alex could only follow in her wake.

Laughter and camaraderie filled the air. He saw the couples mingling, the happiness in their eyes, and a part of him yearned for that kind of connection. Yet his own fears and insecurities held him back, whispering that he could never measure up to those around him.

Sarah caught his eye. Her smile was warm and genuine. A wave of reassurance washed over him.

Unlike his colleagues, she didn't force him to talk. She let him stand beside her in silence. She kept a hand on his biceps or leaned into him. Though it was Alex who felt like he was the one being supported.

Then came the big test. Alex had been clocking Commander Mitchell since he stepped out of the car. As the man himself approached, Alex couldn't help but feel a sense of anticipation. He had hoped that Sarah's genuine warmth and charm would make a lasting impression on his boss, and as their conversation unfolded, it became evident that his hopes were not in vain.

Commander Mitchell's eyes sparkled with interest as he engaged in conversation with Sarah. He listened intently as she shared her involvement in the community, her dedication to various volunteer organizations, and her genuine passion for making a positive impact on people's lives one bouquet at a time. It was clear that Sarah was integral to the fabric of the town, and her influence resonated with Commander Mitchell.

"You've found yourself quite a remarkable woman," the commander said while Sarah engaged in conversation with his wife. "Sarah's dedication to the community is truly commendable. It seems that she has a way of bringing out the best in people."

It was true. Especially with Alex himself. She hadn't made him more talkative or sociable. But being around her, being with her, made the last two social outings endurable. He knew he would not have even gone if it weren't for her steadying presence at his side.

"I was wrong about you, Alex. You have the

potential to be a true leader here. With Sarah by your side, I can see a future where you both contribute to the betterment of this base and community."

Those words of praise were as good as a promotion. He'd done it. They'd done it.

So why did a sense of doom settle over Alex's shoulders for the rest of the picnic?

CHAPTER NINE

The drive home from the company picnic was filled with an uncharacteristic silence. It wasn't like the silence of their drive over, which had been a comfortable, companionable silence. This one was loud, with things left unsaid.

Sarah's mind raced with a whirlwind of thoughts and doubts, causing her heart to sink with each passing moment. She couldn't shake the feeling that something was wrong. That perhaps she had done something wrong. Maybe said something wrong to someone.

Her gaze drifted to Alex, who seemed lost in his own thoughts, his brows furrowed ever so slightly. Was he disappointed in her? Was he regretting their agreement? If her performance as his fake girlfriend during the event had fallen short of his expectations, she had no idea how to fix it. The thought weighed heavily on her, causing a knot of anxiety to form in the pit of her stomach.

Sarah's mind conjured up scenarios of how their charade might have unraveled. What if someone had discovered the truth about their fake relationship? What if Commander Mitchell had called Alex out on his alleged deception? A surge of worry washed over her, and she bit her lip anxiously.

The silence in the car became unbearable. But it took until they were parked outside her house for Sarah to muster the courage to break it. Her voice trembled slightly as she spoke, uncertainty lacing her words. "Alex, is everything okay?"

"Yeah," he sighed. "He's going to offer me that promotion."

"That's great."

So why wasn't he smiling?

Alex turned his gaze toward her, his eyes reflecting a mixture of surprise and concern. He reached out to gently grasp her hand, providing a comforting anchor amidst her growing fears. "It's all because of you."

Sarah's heart fluttered at his reassurance, her anxiety momentarily eased. She squeezed his hand in gratitude, appreciating the warmth and support he offered. "I was just worried that something had gone wrong. That we had been caught or..." She trailed off, her voice faltering.

"No, nothing like that. The truth is, I'm still processing everything, including the offer from Commander Mitchell. It's a lot to take in, and my mind tends to overanalyze things."

"This is what you wanted, right?" Sarah spoke the words, but all she could feel was the warmth of his fingers as they entwined with hers.

"He thinks it's real, our relationship. They all do. I'm not sure if we can break up."

A sense of relief washed over Sarah as she realized that her fears were unfounded. But also the realization that this thing between her and Alex wouldn't be over just yet. The weight that had been pressing upon her lifted, replaced by a renewed sense of hope.

"I mean, I know we have to," he rushed on. "The deal was just two dates. No attachments."

Sarah noticed the tension in his shoulders and the furrow in his brow. She knew he was worrying about something, but she couldn't tell what it was. Did he not want the charade to go on?

She wasn't sure she wanted the answer. Mainly because she knew what her response would be. She wasn't ready for this fake relationship to end. Because ever since he'd come to pick her up the other day for her family reunion, it had started to feel real.

The warm glow of the setting sun bathed the front porch of Sarah's house, casting a soft and gentle light upon her and Alex. They sat with their hands intertwined. They'd been doing that all day. At first it was for show. Then it started to feel natural. Natural enough that they still clung to each other when no one else was around to witness it.

What was between them couldn't be fake. Not if her feelings were real. And the warmth in his palm, the sparks in his eyes told Sarah that he was feeling something too.

Sarah's mind buzzed with a mixture of uncertainty and determination, while her heart longed for the day when their relationship would no longer be a façade. She stole a glance at Alex, his strong profile illuminated by the fading sunlight. His eyes were filled with a mixture of resolve and hesitation, mirroring the emotions swirling within her own heart.

On one hand, the arrangement brought relief, offering respite from her parents' incessant match-making attempts. It provided a shield against their expectations and allowed her to forge her own path. But on the other hand, she wondered if prolonging the charade would only deepen her emotional entanglement with Alex, making it harder to separate their genuine feelings from the pretend.

She knew deep down that their connection was more than just a ruse, but she also feared the consequences of allowing their emotions to take over. The line between fiction and reality was becoming increasingly blurred.

Like now, when Alex's gaze dipped to her lips. If this were an actual date, it was the clear signal that a goodnight kiss was incoming. But Alex pulled back.

When he did, Sarah saw a sight that made her eyes sore. Walking down the street, hand in hand, were her cousin and her ex-boyfriend.

Janet was a second cousin, which meant that she really should have ceded the territory of the reunion to Sarah, who was the eldest grandchild.

But family was family, and she couldn't put up a barrier for blood.

Her neighborhood block was a different story. Janet didn't even live in town. She lived in the next town over. So what reason she could have possibly had to saunter down Sarah's street with her ex-boyfriend Sarah couldn't fathom. She couldn't even be made to care.

All Sarah knew was that she was done being used and made a fool of. Luckily for her, she still had access to a drop-dead gorgeous soldier who was showing clear signs of wanting to kiss her. She just needed to give him a shove in the right direction.

She tugged Alex closer to her, needing to feel his reassuring presence. Before she could think too much about it, Sarah leaned in and kissed him, savoring the warmth of his lips against hers. It felt so right to be in his arms, and for a moment, she forgot about everything else.

CHAPTER TEN

Alex was caught off guard when Sarah tugged him close and kissed him. For the first time in his life, he was completely unprepared for what to expect, and then how to handle it.

At first, when she grabbed his shirt collar, the fleeting thought crossed Alex's mind that she needed to whisper something discreetly. No matter that they were alone inside his car with the windows up.

In the instant that her breath touched his lips, his tactical mind short-circuited, giving him a respite from the constant state of alertness that had become his norm. As she pressed herself closer to him, eliminating the distance between the driver's and passenger seats, Alex's thoughts shifted from tactics to emotions, from analyzing potential threats to savoring the tenderness and depth of the connection they shared.

For once, he embraced the vulnerability that came with letting someone in, finding solace in the notion that love could be a powerful force. It was a risk, a leap of faith into uncharted territory, but one that seemed worth taking. He allowed himself to surrender to the moment without any plan of escape.

Before her lips met his, Alex's thoughts converged on a singular realization: Sarah's intentions were rooted in the desire for genuine connection, a longing to bridge the gap between them and transcend this notion of pretend. It was real for her, too. He knew that he couldn't resist the magnetic pull any longer.

And so he let her take charge, knowing if he were to lead, he just might well botch it. He likely would overthink it. He definitely would have hesitated to give the order for the mission to go forward.

Sarah's lips felt soft and warm against his. The first touch was a bomb going off in his head. The usual calculations and threat assessments that dominated his thoughts were momentarily eclipsed by a surge of desire and longing. The world around them faded into the background, leaving only the two of them sitting there, their connection palpable. Instead of running away or ducking for cover, he leaped into the fray.

Alex wrapped his arms around her waist, pulling her even closer to him. His instincts urging him to protect her, even in the midst of this seemingly harmless moment. Her small gasp made his mind forget its usual vigilance as he was captivated by the magnetic pull between them.

Leaning in, Alex's fingers gently cupped Sarah's face. His heart thundered in his chest, a mix of exhilaration and trepidation flooding his senses. The touch of her lips against his was both electric and tender, igniting a fire within him that he hadn't known existed.

Time stood still as their lips moved in perfect synchrony. They marched to the beat of drums that only they could hear. Alex allowed himself to let go, to embrace what came with genuine connection. He immersed himself in the sweetness of the kiss, savoring the taste of Sarah, as if memorizing every sensation.

For those fleeting moments, the world made sense. The chaos of his thoughts was silenced by the sheer power of their connection. Alex realized that the risks he had spent his life calculating and preparing for paled in comparison to the risk of denying himself the peace and happiness he found in Sarah's arms.

As they reluctantly pulled away, a soft sigh escaped from Alex's lips, his forehead resting gently against Sarah's. He found himself desperately clinging to the moment, his mind racing to find a way to preserve what they had. For the first time, he allowed himself to acknowledge the depth of his feelings, understanding that the status quo could no longer suffice.

In that stolen moment of tenderness, Alex's world shifted. The unyielding walls he had erected around his heart began to crumble, replaced by the undeniable truth that he never wanted to stop kissing Sarah, to let go of the warmth and joy she brought into his life.

As Alex and Sarah sat in the car, their stolen moment was interrupted by the sound of a throat being cleared. Alex's senses snapped back to full alertness. His eyes darted towards the source of the noise, his body instinctively tensing in preparation for potential danger.

"Alex." Sarah's voice was breathy, as it should be. She'd just been kissed stupid. "This is Bernie."

Bernie? That name sounded familiar. Alex never forgot details, but he too had just been kissed stupid.

Sarah was already out of the car. Alex was still held by his seatbelt. He scrambled to be released from the device and rounded the car to face this threat. Though Sarah seemed ready to fight, not back down.

Bernie. Sarah's ex-boyfriend. The realization hit him like a bolt of lightning.

"So this is your new guy?" Her ex sneered as he gestured to Alex. "I see you're trying new things like PDA."

"What can I say? He can't keep his hands off me. And I feel the same way."

Alex was an excellent reader of body language. Sarah's body language did not signal affection. It shouted aggression. Her shoulders were tense, her fists balled. Her head was tilted up like she was expecting to take it on the chin.

There were two things Alex knew. The first was that if this guy took even a step closer to Sarah, he would wind up flat on his back. The second thing Alex knew was that that kiss had not been for his benefit. It had been for Bernie's.

"I'm so glad you've moved on, cuz," said a petite woman at Bernie's side. "We tried to give you some space at the reunion. That's why we didn't show."

"Oh? Is that why, Janet? I thought I heard something about trouble in paradise."

"Oh, no." Janet smiled sweetly. "They must have been referring to Bernie's last relationship. This one will go the distance."

Janet patted Bernie's chest. She looked up into the man's eyes adoringly. Bernie's gaze remained fixed on Sarah.

"Good for you," said Sarah. "The two of you deserve each other."

"We're headed to Aunt Cathy's," said Janet. "She's teaching me her potato salad recipe tonight. You know, she only does that for the married women, so…"

Janet let the last word linger.

"Don't wanna be late." Janet gave Bernie a tug. It took the man a few tugs to get moving. His gaze never left Sarah.

When Alex and Sarah were finally alone again, she gave her body a shake that a wet dog would have approved of. Then she turned and faced Alex.

"I'm sorry about that," she said.

Alex remained quiet. He hadn't been sorry. As they stood outside Sarah's house, Alex felt a sense of sadness wash over him. The kiss they'd shared had been incredible, but it had also brought up a lot of emotions he wasn't quite sure he was ready to deal with. He knew he was falling for Sarah, but he was also afraid to admit his feelings.

"I think it's better if we end this," he said, his voice barely above a whisper.

"Wait… Alex… I…" Sarah looked at him, her eyes searching his face for any sign of hesitation.

"You don't have to tell anyone that we broke up. You can keep the farce going for as long as you need. But I think I'm going to be pretty busy at work with my new responsibilities."

"Yes… Of course…" Sarah took a step closer to him, her hand reaching out to touch his arm. "Still friends, right?"

Alex's heart swelled with emotion at her words, but he couldn't shake the feeling that a proposition like that would only come with pain. At first, he'd thought he'd end up hurting her. Now he realized he was the one in danger. So for the first time in his life, Alex told a tactical lie.

"Yeah. Still friends."

CHAPTER ELEVEN

Sarah sat on the couch. The television blared as her family gathered for their favorite Food Network cooking competition. Chefs who were clearly long-time friends smack-talked each other as they sliced and diced. Sarah heard none of it.

Her mind kept drifting back to the kiss she'd shared with Alex. The imprint of his lips lingered on hers, creating a sensation that she couldn't easily forget. It had been a simple act, meant to deceive the world around them, but its impact had been far from ordinary.

She replayed the moment in her mind, each detail etched vividly in her thoughts. The way their bodies had collided. The tender way Alex had reached out to bring her closer to him.

The world had blurred around her as their lips met, a surge of warmth and desire coursing through her veins. In that singular moment, time stood still. All her worries and doubts had dissolved into oblivion. It had been a kiss that had left her breathless, a kiss that spoke of something deeper, something real.

It had awakened a dormant part of her heart, stirring emotions she had long buried beneath layers of caution. With each passing second, her feelings for Alex grew more undeniable, like a flame that refused to be extinguished.

But as she sat now, lost in the rapture of that stolen kiss, a pang of uncertainty seeped into her thoughts. She questioned the authenticity of her feelings, reminding herself that the kiss had been part of their charade, a performance to fool the world.

Still friends.

Doubts gnawed at her, like a persistent voice in her mind. She'd heard it in his voice. Those words had been a lie. Sarah knew in her heart that she would likely never see Alex again.

At least not the Alex she'd seen over the past two days. The one who had been on her side, no matter what. The one who had held her hand and lent her his support. The one who had stood united with her to get her the thing she desired most.

And what was that thing? To not be badgered into dating. To not be nagged into finding a husband.

Still friends.

The more she thought about Alex, the more she felt drawn to him. He was different from anyone she had ever dated before. He was kind, under-standing, and patient with her. And that kiss had felt so real, so passionate.

Sarah was so lost in thought that she didn't even hear the knock on her door until it sounded again, more insistent this time. No one else in her family moved. They were so engrossed in the elim-ination round of the two top chefs that they didn't even blink at the third round of knocking.

Neither was Sarah. She knew that knock. She almost didn't get up to answer it. But in the end, she knew he wouldn't leave until he was acknowledged.

She opened the door, and there he was. Her ex stood on her doorstep with a bouquet of flowers.

"Wrong house, Bernie. Aunt Cathy lives around the block. That's where your fiancée is making you potato salad."

Her ex looked at her with pleading eyes. "Sarah, please, can we talk?"

He looked remorseful and miserable, and Sarah couldn't care less.

She crossed her arms and glared at him. "What could you possibly have to say to me that I would want to hear?"

"I've been miserable without you," he said. "Then I saw you with that guy and I realized that what we had was real. I want you back, Sarah."

"Let me get this straight. You saw me with another man, and now you want me back?"

"No, that's not what I meant. What I mean is-"

"I can't believe you have the nerve to come here and ask for me back after everything you did."

"I made a mistake."

"Does Janet know that? Have you had this conversation with her? Or are you here to try to cheat on her with me?"

Bernie sighed as though she was the one being unreasonable.

"Okay, Bernie."

"Okay?" He perked up.

"Yeah, okay. You want me back? Let's go over to Aunt Cathy's now and tell Janet together."

"Right now?"

"Right now."

"That's kind of cruel. We could wait until tomorrow. Maybe go for a ride in my-"

Sarah slammed the door on him and leaned her back against it, feeling emotionally drained. The kiss with Alex, her feelings for him, and now her ex trying to come back into her life...it was all too much to handle.

She stood in the doorway, her heart still racing from her encounter with her ex-boyfriend. She closed the door firmly, shutting him out of her life for good. Before she turned, she noted the silence in the room behind her. The cooking competition was muted. Her family's attention was now focused solely on her.

Her mother, with an eyebrow arched, broke the silence. "Can you believe the nerve of that boy?"

Sarah opened her mouth and closed it. Her mother had never spoken a single ill word of Bernie. She was still hoping to get him back as her son-in-law.

"I have half a mind to call his mother and let her know just how poorly he's behaved," she continued.

"He's certainly not welcome inside this house again," said her father. "And I won't be lending him any worms on this weekend's fishing trip."

"Good for you, sis. You deserve better than that jerk. I'm Team Alex, all the way."

"Same here." Her mother clapped her hands together. "Alex is such a gentleman. He's going to make a perfect addition to this family. And oh, the grandbabies."

Sarah reached out to cling to the back of the recliner. Her family was giving her whiplash from the speed with which they'd gone from Team Bernie to Team Alex. But had they once been Team Sarah?

"You need to lock that one down, Sarah," her mother was saying. "A summer wedding would be so lovely."

"Wedding? We went on two dates. And they weren't even real."

The words were out there before Sarah could take them back. Her family stared at her in confusion. Sarah decided not to clarify.

"What do you mean not real?" asked her father. "I saw the way that young man looked at you. He's clearly taken by you."

"He wasn't taken by me," Sarah sighed, but the words felt heavy on her tongue. "We were faking it. He needed a girlfriend to impress his boss so that he could get a promotion at work. And I just wanted to get you guys off my back about dating and marriage and have some peace."

Sarah's family's expressions softened as they exchanged remorseful glances. Well, her mother's and father's did. Her sister continued to smirk, clearly thinking the whole situation was hilarious and would likely post about it on social media later… or right now.

"Sarah, we're so sorry for constantly pressuring you about dating and marriage," said her father. "We didn't realize how much it affected you. Can you find it in your heart to forgive us?"

Sarah took a moment to absorb this heartfelt apology. She could see the genuine remorse in her parents' eyes. She knew their intentions had always been rooted in love, even if their approach had been misguided. With a warm smile, she nodded.

"Of course, Mom and Dad. I understand that you wanted what you thought was best for me. But I need you to realize that I might be the best judge of that."

Her father reached out, placing a comforting hand on her shoulder. "We love you, Sarah, and we want nothing more than your happiness. We'll support you in whatever decisions you make moving forward."

He opened his arms, and Sarah came into them. But just as she was beginning to bask in the warmth of their newfound understanding, her mother couldn't help but interject, her voice filled with excitement.

"You know, Sarah, if what you had with Alex looked so real, maybe it's a sign that there's something more there. Have you ever considered giving it a real chance? It didn't look fake at all to me."

"It wasn't real," said Sarah. "It was all for show."

Still friends. Sarah wasn't even sure if they were that anymore. But she did know that what she was feeling for him was far beyond the boundaries of friendship, and honestly, that scared her more than anything.

Her mother stepped forward, taking both of

Sarah's hands in hers. "Maybe it started out that way, but we all saw the way you two were together. You should go talk to him, see if there's something there."

CHAPTER TWELVE

As Alex walked into the office, he couldn't help but feel anxious. He was feeling down after breaking it off with Sarah, and he hadn't gotten any sleep because of his anxiety. He knew the only thing that would calm him down would be to solve a complex problem that dealt with numbers.

Numbers weren't emotional. Numbers didn't make him question. They were straightforward. Though not actually the colors black and white, they were a binary choice.

But as he sat at his desk running his calculations, he couldn't focus on any of the outcomes. All he could think about was how much he missed Sarah and how much he wanted to be with her. He realized that being with her made him feel calm and supported, and he needed that now more than ever.

"Alex, I wanted to talk to you about something," his boss said.

"The new project? Yes, I'll have it done in just another hour or so, sir."

"No, not the new project. I wanted to invite you over to dinner."

"Dinner, sir?"

"Yes, my wife was very taken with Sarah. We'd love to have you over this weekend for a relaxing time out on the back porch. Hopefully, she'll bring over some of that potato salad she raved about."

Alex felt his heart sink at the mention of Sarah's name. He had been trying to keep his mind off of her, but it seemed like fate was determined to keep them connected.

"It didn't work out between us," Alex said, his voice softening.

"It didn't?" His boss looked at him quizzically. "That's a shame. I thought you two were perfect for each other."

"Sir, I'm really not comfortable about bringing my relationship into the work world. I need there to be a division between the two so that I can be most effective."

Commander Mitchell nodded, but Alex could tell that he wasn't entirely convinced.

"I've been sitting here for hours trying to solve this problem, but all I'm doing is thinking about Sarah."

Alex could feel his heart pounding in his chest. He knew that his feelings for her were genuine, but he didn't think hers were for him. She'd only kissed him to get back at her cheating ex. But could Alex truly be upset when they'd entered into this agreement to lie to everyone else? It wasn't her fault that it had started to feel real to him. It wasn't her fault that he now wanted more than they had initially signed up for.

"I'm truly sorry things didn't work out for the two of you," the commander was saying. "Not because of my beliefs in workers putting down roots in this community, but because I really thought I saw something between the two of you. I'm not usually wrong about these things. Are you sure you can't work it out?"

"I don't know." Alex didn't want to talk about his emotions anymore. Already he was feeling out of control. "But I can assure you that my passion and dedication to this job has never wavered, even now that I'm going through a tough time."

His boss nodded slowly, seeming to accept Alex's explanation.

"I deserve this promotion, and I'm going to work my hardest to prove it to you. Who I'm dating shouldn't have bearing on that."

"I hear you." The commander rested a hand on Alex's shoulder. "But sometimes, letting go of someone you love can be the biggest mistake of all."

Alex watched the man walk out of his office. But one word that he said lingered in the open air. Love. Did Alex love Sarah?

It was too soon.

Wasn't it?

He'd thought he was doing the right thing by not holding on to her. But what if he'd miscalculated? What if letting her go would prove catastrophic?

The only thing Alex knew for certain was that he needed to see her again, to talk to her and explain his feelings. He couldn't let her slip away without giving her all of the information. She deserved that much, at least.

CHAPTER THIRTEEN

*S*arah hadn't slept a wink last night. She put on a ton of concealer trying to hide that fact as the morning light seeped into the bathroom window. For the first time in her life, she was going to take her family up on their meddling advice.

No, she wasn't going to propose marriage to Alex. But she was going to propose that they stop faking it and see if they could have a real relationship.

Her family being her family, they'd insisted on driving her. The car hummed along the road as Sarah, her mother, her father, and her sister embarked on the journey to the military base.

Tension mingled with anticipation in the air, making the atmosphere palpable. Sarah's mind buzzed with thoughts of how to approach the conversation with Alex, while her family seemed equally absorbed in their own thoughts.

Her mother, always the one to break the silence, leaned forward from the backseat, her eyes sparkling with mischievousness. "All right, Sarah, I have a foolproof plan to get Alex to date you for real," she declared with a grin.

"Oh, here we go. Mom's Matchmaking Advice 101," said her sister.

"Step one," her mother began.

"No, Mom," said Sarah. "You've done enough driving me here and encouraging me. Now, stay in the car and let me handle this myself."

Her mother's lips pressed together as though she were going to start to lecture Sarah, but her husband wrapped an arm around her. Sarah knew that arm served to hold her in her seat, not to be affectionate.

Miraculously, Sarah climbed out of the car with no one following her. Her heart raced with anticipation as she made her way inside the military base. The lack of sleep seemed inconsequential compared to the surge of emotions propelling her forward. Today, she was determined to follow her instincts and take a leap of faith, guided by the newfound clarity she had gained.

As the sun cast its golden rays across the horizon, Sarah entered the base, her footsteps echoing in the quiet morning air. She made her way to the designated area where she hoped to find Alex. Each passing moment intensified her resolve and steeled her nerves, even as her mind raced with thoughts of what she was about to do.

Sarah's heart skipped a beat when she saw Alex standing at the edge of a lively gathering. By the looks of it, it was someone's birthday party. Alex had told her he usually avoided things like this. But here he was, participating.

Standing on the edge, but at least he was near the circle of being social.

His brows furrowed slightly as he kept his gaze fixed on his phone, seemingly lost in his thoughts. Before she could dwell on his demeanor, her phone suddenly rang, breaking the momentary silence.

Looking down, she saw that it was him.

The sound of Alex's voice washed over her,

carrying a sense of determination and sincerity. He spoke with a hint of nervousness, yet his words were resolute. "Sarah?"

"Alex?"

"Hi."

"Hello."

There was a pause as she watched him. He looked nervous and uncertain. Then resolute.

"Would you like to have dinner with me tonight?" he asked.

"I'd like-"

"Wait. Before you answer, I want you to know that it would be a date. A real date. With me."

Sarah's heart beat wildly. Her grin stretched so broadly that her lips began to hurt.

Alex sighed heavily. That's when she realized she hadn't answered him.

"Yes. Yes, I'd love to go on a real date with you. I want to stop pretending. I want to try and make this real between us."

"You do?"

Sarah noted that she could hear him clearly. In the room, not on the phone. All conversation and birthday singing had stopped. The crowd was looking between him and Sarah as though they were witnessing a tennis match.

Sarah's heart swelled with a mixture of emotions. It was as if the universe had conspired to align their thoughts and desires. She took a deep breath, her voice steady as she responded, "Look up, Alex."

There was a brief pause on the other end of the line, followed by a sharp intake of breath. Sarah's eyes met Alex's as he finally looked up from his phone, his gaze locking with hers. The world around them seemed to fade away, leaving only the two of them standing there in that moment.

The corners of Alex's lips curved into a heart-warming smile, his eyes lighting up with a newfound hope. In that instant, Sarah could see the unspoken words reflected in his gaze, the depth of his feelings mirrored in his expression.

"What are you waiting for?" said her mother from behind her. "Go and kiss the man. It'll be great practice for the wedding vows."

Sarah slowly approached him, her heart pounding with a mix of anticipation and joy. The distance between them closed with each step, their connection growing stronger. And when their eyes finally met, time seemed to stand still, the bustling celebration of his colleagues fading into the background.

The cheers and encouragement of Sarah's family filled the air, creating an electric atmosphere that seemed to amplify the anticipation. The moment hung suspended in time as Sarah and Alex stood together, their eyes locked in a shared understanding.

In that charged moment, Alex's lips gently met Sarah's. The kiss held a depth of emotion, a merging of their desires and the validation of their feelings for each other. It was a kiss that signified the end of pretense and the beginning of something real.

As their lips parted, a collective cheer erupted, celebrating the newfound connection between Sarah and Alex. The joyous applause filled the space, wrapping around them like a warm embrace. Sarah couldn't help but smile, her heart brimming with happiness and a sense of fulfillment.

Gazing into Alex's eyes, she found a reflection of her own emotions—hope, tenderness, and an undeniable spark that transcended any previous doubts. In that shared moment, their relationship transformed from a charade to an authentic bond, built on trust, understanding, and the courage to take a leap of faith.

. . .

Don't miss the next book in the Honor Valley
Romances!

The fiercest battles are often won one page at a time.

When former military language specialist
Mason Turner returns home to recover from the
physical and emotional scars of his service, he
seeks solace in the quiet haven of the local library.
There, he meets the warm and understanding
librarian Grace, who captures his heart with her
genuine care and unwavering support.

Facing the threat of the library's beloved
reading program being cut, Grace turns to Mason
for help, tapping into his unique skills and passion
for language. As they battle external challenges and
confront their own emotional wounds, Mason and
Grace learn that the power of love can overcome
the darkest moments and lead to the brightest
future.

**Soldier's Courage is a heartwarming small-
town military romance that explores the power
of love, growth, and healing. With the *Beauty and***

the Beast trope, wounded hero, and the power of love to heal, this story will sweep you away and leave you rooting for Grace and Mason's happily ever after.

Soldier's Promise

Soldier's Courage

Soldier's Embrace

Soldier's Triumph

Soldier's Protection

The Brides of Purple Heart

On His Bended Knee

Hand Over His Heart

Offering His Arm

His Permanent Scar

Having His Back

In Over His Head

Always On His Mind

Every Step He Takes

In His Good Hands

Light Up His Life

Strength to Stand

His Grace Under Pressure

The Rangers of Purple Heart

The Rancher takes his Convenient Bride

The Rancher takes his Best Friend's Sister

The Rancher takes his Runaway Bride

The Rancher takes his Star Crossed Love

The Rancher takes his Love at First Sight

The Rancher takes his Last Chance at Love

The Silver Star Ranch Romances

His Pledge to Honor

His Pledge to Cherish

His Pledge to Protect

His Pledge to Obey

His Pledge to Have

His Pledge to Hold

a Flying Cross Ranch Romance

His Vow to Love

His Vow to Treasure

His Vow to Adore

His Vow to Trust

His Vow to Respect

His Vow to Defend

Bronze Star Ranch Romance

His Duty to Serve

His Duty to Accept

His to Fulfill

www.ingramcontent.com/pod-product-compliance
Lightning Source LLC
Chambersburg PA
CBHW022028150726
47990CB00002B/867